Earl was born with one enormous front tooth,

and as Earl grew that tooth grew too.

...and at an alarming rate!

Earl Joins the Circus

In Memory of Louanne Scheber
Always and ever the Best.

Copyright Scheber 2005
All rights reserved

Published by Make Me a Story Press (MMASP)
P. O. Box 151, Watseka, IL 60970

TM

Library of Congress Control Number: 2005902994

ISBN 9781878847010

Printed in China First Edition, June 2005

Something new was

in the air.

Earl saw the new sign,

and he read it.

The sign said, "The Circus is Coming to Town."

Instantly, Earl had an idea.

*Earl's idea was
so exciting
he had to
recurl himself
twice that night...*

...before he could fall asleep.

Before all the tents were up,

Earl went to see the ringmaster

(he's the boss).

Earl wanted to be
a star.

He could already see
his name in lights.

Earl did flips,

The boss simply wasn't impressed.

Earl's hopes sank completely, when the ringmaster said, "Kid, we have people who already do those tricks."

Earl hung his head to walk away
when it happened.

Earl tripped on his own tooth...

By the time the tents were up, Earl had signed a contract.

He was the new circus clown.

What fun it was!

*In one act, Earl was
a spinning wheel.*

Earl and Stiltman teamed up
for another act,

and Earl bounced
like a basketball.

Between shows
Earl tried on
other costumes.

Putting on
make-up
tickled.

What great
disguises he
discovered!

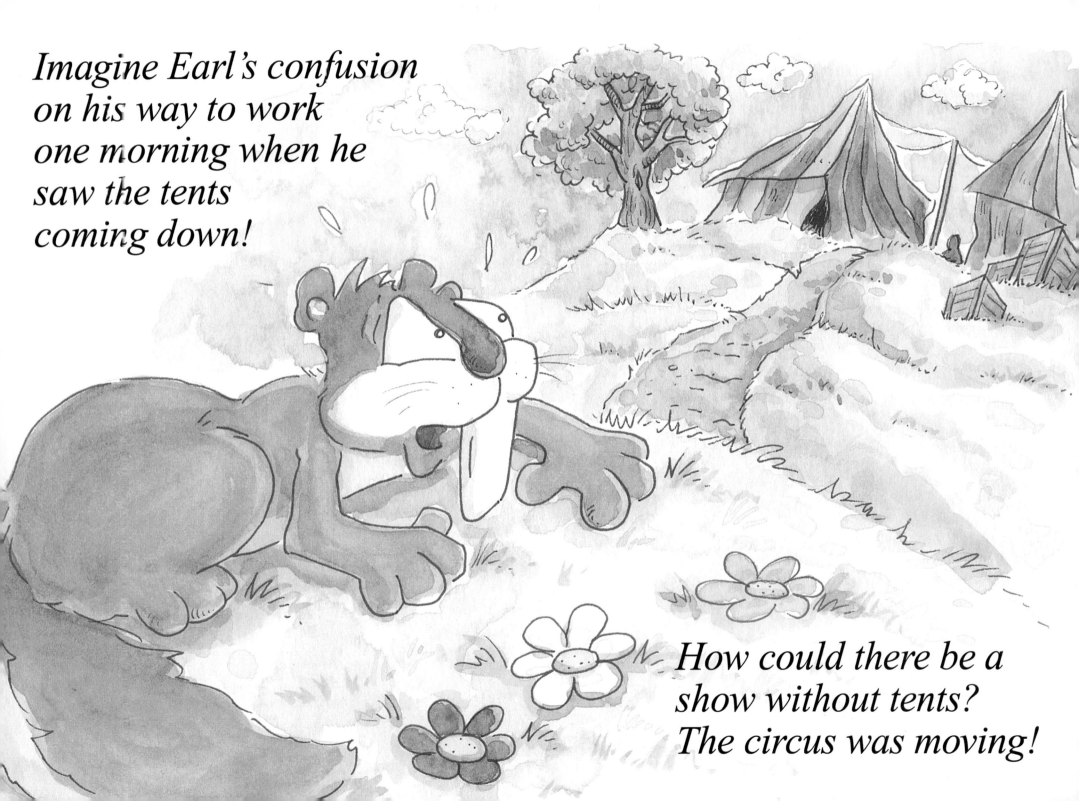

Imagine Earl's confusion on his way to work one morning when he saw the tents coming down!

How could there be a show without tents? The circus was moving!

Earl positively couldn't leave home.

The boss was laughing when he handed the contract to Earl.

Then Sid turned the contract over.
Was there more? Yes!

Earl had to perform,
but only when the
circus was in Earl's
hometown...

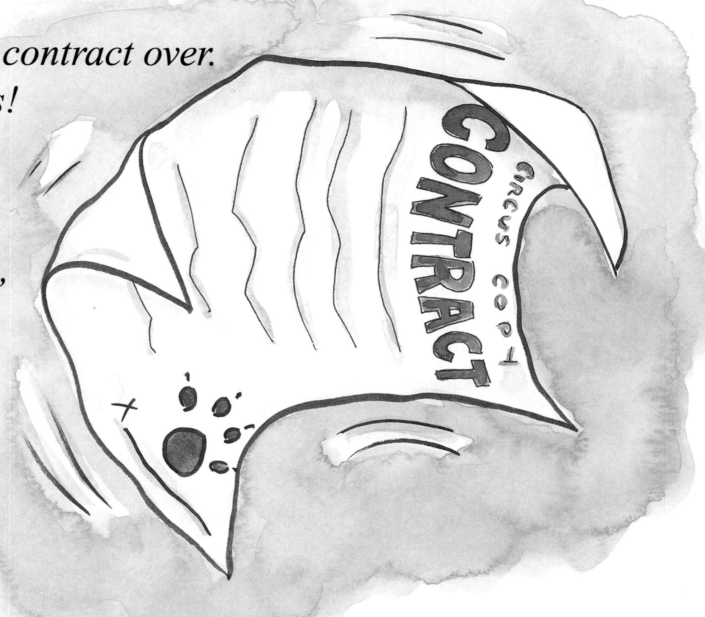

...providing he wanted to,
that is.

*The ringmaster smiled, and before
Earl could thank his true friend,*

The End